THIS
BOOK
BELONGS

TO _____

GROLIER
B O O K S

LEPRECHAUNS ON THE LOOSE

An Adventure in Ireland

Developed by The Walt Disney Company in conjunction with Nancy Hall, Inc.
ISBN: 0-7172-8224-4
Grolier Books is a division of Grolier Enterprises, Inc.

"Yes siree!" Donald said to Daisy as he happily packed his suitcase. "A vacation in Ireland is just what I need to turn my luck around. I'll catch a leprechaun, and then I'll be rich and all my troubles will be over!"

"Now, Donald," said Daisy in a firm voice. "You and I both know there is no such thing as a leprechaun. I don't want you spending our whole vacation looking for something that doesn't exist."

Donald just shrugged and gave the room one last look to make sure that he wasn't forgetting anything. He didn't realize that he was taking along two extra passengers. Chip and Dale, hoping for an adventure of their own, had made themselves comfortable in Donald's carry-on bag.

Donald and Daisy called a taxi and left for the airport. When they were finally seated on the plane, Donald introduced himself to the man beside him.

"It's lovely to meet you," said the man. "My name is Paddy O'Shea."

"With a name like that, you must be from Ireland," said Donald. "Do you know if it's true that if you catch a leprechaun, he must tell you where he has hidden his gold?"

With that Paddy let out a roar of laughter. "Don't tell me that you believe in the little people!" he said.

"As a matter of fact, I do," said Donald confidently. "And that's why I'm going to Ireland."

"In that case," said Paddy, "you'll want to hear everything there is to know about the subject." Paddy told Donald one leprechaun tale after another. By the time the airplane landed at Shannon Airport, they had become good friends.

"Instead of staying in a hotel, why don't you both come home with me?" Paddy asked Donald and Daisy. "My wife just loves to have company. I'll give her a call and let her know you're coming."

Donald and Daisy piled into Paddy's car and headed toward Paddy's house.

"Now I see why they call Ireland the Emerald Isle!" said Daisy, as she stared through the window at the lovely green landscape. "Everything is exactly the same color as an emerald jewel."

Paddy's wife, Colleen, greeted them at the door and introduced their daughter, Erin. Colleen led them to the dining table for a meal of Irish stew and soda bread.

"You know," said Paddy, "I raise horses for a living, and I'm taking a trip this week to look for a new mare. Why don't you two come along? That way I can show you the sights."

"Great idea!" said Donald.

"We couldn't find a better guide!" Daisy agreed.

While the others were eating, Chip and Dale hopped out of Donald's bag and went off to do some exploring. In baby Erin's room they found some doll clothes that were just their size!

The next morning Chip and Dale hopped into Paddy's car as he left with Donald and Daisy. Paddy drove to Bunratty village, where Donald and Daisy went on a tour of the town. After a long day, they met Paddy for dinner at Bunratty Castle. There they were served by people who were wearing historical costumes.

Donald accidentally dropped his dinner roll under the table. When he bent down to pick it up, he saw an amazing sight.

"Leprechauns!" he shouted. Donald began crawling under the tables, chasing the little elves.

All the dinner guests held their plates as Donald scrambled frantically through the dining hall. By the time he returned to his place, all his food was cold.

"I hope I didn't cause too much trouble," Donald said, his face turning bright red.

The next day, Paddy took them to the Pony Show at Clifden in County Galway. "This is a fine-looking animal!" said Paddy as he inspected a shiny black horse.

Just at that moment, Donald spied a little leprechaun darting by the horse's hooves. "I'll catch you this time!" Donald cried.

The horse began to bob its head and stamp its feet in alarm. Donald searched high and low, but he returned to Paddy and Daisy empty-handed.

"Don't tell me," said Paddy, laughing at Donald. "The little people are up to their tricks again."

"Oh, Donald," groaned Daisy, rolling her eyes. "Haven't you learned your lesson yet?"

Donald just muttered to himself. "Those leprechauns won't get away from me next time," he vowed. "Then everyone will see I'm not imagining things."

Later Paddy took Donald and Daisy to a gift shop in Galway.

"Ireland is known for its beautiful glass and handknit sweaters," said Daisy, turning to Donald. "Let's buy one of these crystal vases as a present for Grandma Duck."

But Donald wasn't listening. He thought he saw a flash of green among the crystal. "Did you see something over there?" he asked Daisy excitedly.

"Not here!" warned Daisy under her breath. "This is no place to start trouble. You could break something!"

"Don't worry," said Donald confidently. Very, very carefully, Donald looked inside vases and behind glasses, but there was not a leprechaun in sight.

The next day Paddy took Daisy and Donald on a side trip to a place called Slea Head.

"This looks like a great place to catch leprechauns," thought Donald. This time he had brought along a large butterfly net just in case any little people showed up.

"What are those buildings over there?" asked Daisy.

"Those are ancient houses, well over a thousand years old," said Paddy. "They're called beehive huts."

But Donald wasn't paying any attention. He was too busy looking behind every beehive hut for leprechauns.

Afterwards, Paddy took Donald and Daisy to look at the famous Blarney Stone.

"It says here that if you kiss the Blarney Stone, you'll be able to convince anyone of anything," read Daisy from her guide book.

"I'll go first," Donald suggested. "Maybe then they'll believe me when I say I've seen a leprechaun," he said to himself. As he tried to reach the stone, he caught a glimpse of a little green cap.

"Leprechauns!" shouted Donald, struggling to get up.

"Your eyes are playing tricks on you, my boy," said Paddy.

"I saw two leprechauns, I tell you!" Donald insisted.

"I think you had better try to kiss the Blarney Stone," said Daisy, laughing. "You still haven't convinced me!"

Next Paddy and Daisy went to Killarney to look at a horse while Donald went fishing in a nearby lake. Chip and Dale followed Donald to the lake, and hopped in to splash and play.

Donald cast his line into the water and immediately felt a tug.

When Donald excitedly reeled in the line, the only thing he had caught was a little green cap.

"Oh, boy! This definitely belongs to a leprechaun!" Donald said happily. "I finally have my proof. Now everyone will have to believe me."

Donald set the cap down while he got his gear together. He couldn't wait to show off his "catch." But while his back was turned, Dale grabbed the cap.

Donald turned around just in time to see the leprechauns running away. "Oh, no! There were two of them right under my nose!" said Donald, stamping his foot. "And I let them get away!"

Soon Paddy and Daisy drove back to pick him up.
Paddy stopped the car along a country lane just
outside of Tralee. "How about a picnic lunch?" he asked.
"What a beautiful spot!" exclaimed Daisy as she
picked a shamrock.
For Donald, the picnic offered another opportunity to
catch the leprechauns, and off he went to set some traps.

Donald had just finished setting the last trap when he heard a strange rustling sound.

"I've got myself a leprechaun now," he said happily.

As Donald walked toward the sound, he tripped over a log and landed in one of his own traps. In a flash Donald was hanging upside down from a tree.

"Whoops!" Donald cried out. Paddy and Daisy ran over to help Donald. Below him, a sheep bleated loudly.

"Some leprechaun you are," Donald muttered to the sheep.

Finally, in County Limerick, Paddy found the horse he had been looking for, a beautiful mare with a flowing mane.

Paddy told Donald and Daisy that they were in the part of Ireland for which the limerick, a type of nonsense poem, had been named. "In fact, I just made one up for you," he said, turning to Donald. "It goes like this:

"There once was a fine feathered gent
Who saw leprechauns wherever he went.
He spied them in stables,
And underneath tables.
He saw them at every event!"
Donald just smiled politely while Daisy chuckled.
"Just wait," he said to himself. "I'll catch a leprechaun yet!"

The group arrived back at Paddy's house late in the day.

"It looks like your trip was a great success," said Colleen when she saw Paddy leading his horse to the stable.

"We saw some beautiful sights," said Daisy. "Ireland is a lovely country."

"I'm sorry that your search didn't go as well, Donald," said Paddy with a chuckle.

"Maybe I didn't catch a leprechaun," muttered Donald, "but at least I know for sure that they exist."

When Donald and Daisy arrived back in the United
States, Mickey was at the airport to greet them.

"How was your trip?" he asked.

"It was wonderful!" replied Daisy. "But Donald wasted
all his time chasing leprechauns."

Donald didn't even hear Daisy. He was staring straight
ahead. He couldn't believe his eyes! There were the
leprechauns again!

This time everyone saw the "leprechauns." Mickey dashed around some luggage and caught them.

"Are these your wee folk, Donald?" Mickey asked, holding up Chip and Dale.

"Yes," muttered Donald sheepishly. "I guess this means I don't get my pot of gold."

"How about a pot of acorns?" asked Mickey. Everyone roared with laughter. Even Donald couldn't help but smile.

Did You Know...?

There are many different customs and places that make each country special. Do you remember some of the things below from the story?

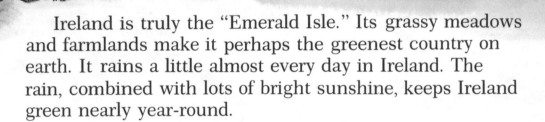

Ireland is truly the "Emerald Isle." Its grassy meadows and farmlands make it perhaps the greenest country on earth. It rains a little almost every day in Ireland. The rain, combined with lots of bright sunshine, keeps Ireland green nearly year-round.

The shamrock is a three-leaved plant that is the national emblem of Ireland. It can be seen on everything from banners to airplanes. Four-leaf clovers, which are similar to shamrocks, are very rare and are thought to bring good luck.

Kissing the Blarney Stone is a popular tourist attraction. To kiss the stone, however, you have to lie on your back and lower your head over the side of Blarney Castle. Be careful, Donald!

Ireland is a fisherman's paradise. Its beautiful rivers and lakes are filled with many kinds of fish, including trout, pike, and salmon.

Leprechauns are said to be mischievous elves that like to play tricks on others. Known as "the little people," they are supposed to be both clever and rich. It is said that leprechauns keep their gold in a pot that they hide at the end of a rainbow. According to legend, if you catch a leprechaun, you can make him take you to his pot of gold.

Horse racing has been a popular sport in Ireland for many years. The Irish invented the steeplechase race, in which horses and riders must leap over ditches, hedges, and stone walls. The race gets its name from the steeple of a church that was at the finish line of the first steeplechase.

The potato is a favorite food in Ireland.
Irish people use potatoes in stews,
and they also enjoy potato soup,
potato pancakes, and potato bread.

The Irish harp is the national musical
instrument of Ireland. It is smaller than other
harps and its frame is made of wood. The
Irish play beautiful folk songs on their harps.

Dia dhuit (dee-a-geech)
means "Hello" in Irish, or
Gaelic (GAY-lik), the first
official language of Ireland.

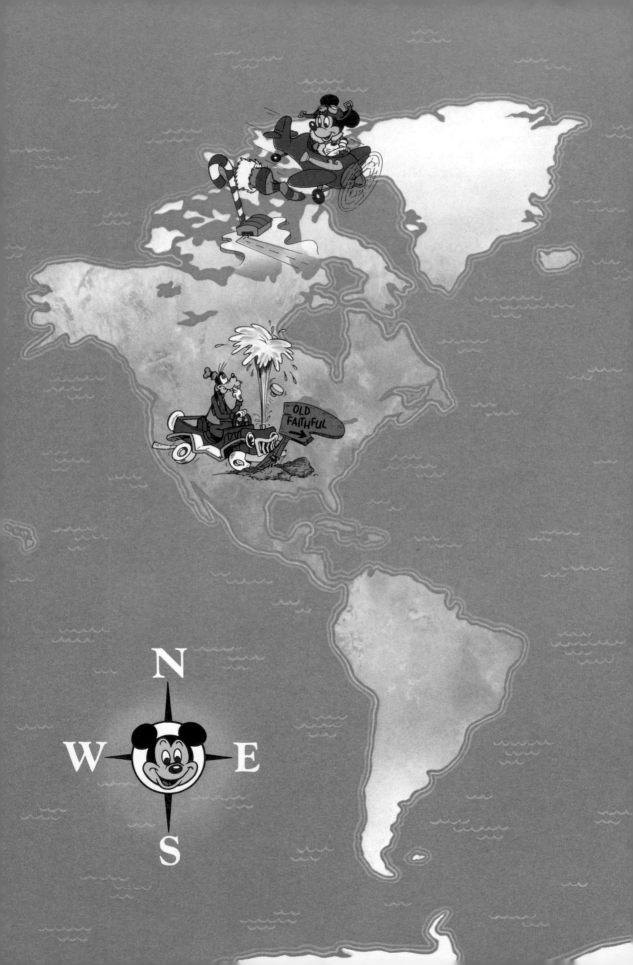